Worm
Pie

Other books in the Shooting Star series:

School Campout
by Becky Citra

The Big Race!
by Sylvia McNicoll

My Homework is in the Mail!
by Becky Citra

Project Disaster
by Sylvia McNicoll

The Lost Locket
by Carol Matas

Abra Kadabra
by Maureen Bayless

Howard's House is Haunted
by Maureen Bayless

Mystery of the Lunchbox Criminal
by Alison Lohans

The Secret Plan
by Alison Lohans

Monsters in the School
by Martyn Godfrey

Worm Pie

Beverly Scudamore

Illustrations by
Susan Gardos

Scholastic Canada Ltd.

For Jenny.

Canadian Cataloguing in Publication Data

Scudamore, Beverly, 1956-
   Worm pie

(Shooting Star)
ISBN 0-590-24978-9

I. Title. II. Series.

PS8587.C82W6 1998   jC813'.54   C96-932165-1
PZ7.S38W0 1998

4 3 2 1   Printed in Canada   7 8 9/9

Contents

Chapter 1

The New Teacher

The principal stood at the front of the classroom. A smile was frozen across her face. I glanced around the room. Our teacher, Mrs. Jay, was missing. Something was definitely wrong.

"Good morning, class," the principal said.

"Good morning, Ms Horton," we answered.

Ms Horton reached into her skirt pocket and brought out a piece of paper. "I have a note from your teacher," she said. She adjusted her glasses and began to read:

Dear Students,

Surprise! My baby was born last night. His name is Joel. He's very small now, but with a little tender loving care, he will grow to be big and strong. Someday soon Joel and I will visit the class.

Your teacher,

Mrs. Jay.

"But, Ms Horton . . . " I blurted out, forgetting to raise my hand.

Ms Horton's smile cracked, and she glared at me. "Forget your manners, Tara?"

Her icy voice sent shivers running up my spine. But I asked my question anyway. "Mrs. Jay was supposed to have her baby in July. It's only June. Is she okay? Is her baby okay?"

"Tara, weren't you listening? I already told you, Mrs. Jay and her baby are fine."

Whew! I sat back in my desk. I would hate it if anything bad ever happened to Mrs. Jay. After all, she was the best teacher at Riverside School. Her warm brown skin and sunny smile could cozy up the whole room. She could even melt Ms Horton, the human iceberg.

Wham! It hit me like a baseball between the eyeballs. Mrs. Jay wasn't coming back! That could only mean one thing — a new teacher!

Ms Horton was saying something to the class. But I didn't hear her. I was too busy thinking about the new teacher. Would she smell flowery? Mrs. Jay smelled like a rose garden. Would she scream a lot? Mrs. Jay never screamed, except for the time when Cory Clue put his earwig collection on her desk, and they all escaped. And, of course, there was the question of homework. Mrs. Jay only gave homework on Tuesdays and Thursdays.

I didn't have to wonder about the new teacher for long because when I looked up, guess who walked in? I blinked once. I blinked twice.

The new teacher was a man. A yellow ball of frizz sat on top of his head. His eyeglasses had yellow lenses in the shape of hexagons. I couldn't stop staring because his eyes looked like two bees buzzing around in a honeycomb.

And that's not all: his shirt had pictures of orange birds flying into each other.

It didn't take long for me to figure out that the new teacher was a GEEK!

Ms Horton straightened her skirt and put on her frosty smile again. "Class, it's my pleasure to introduce Mr. Stanley. He'll be your teacher for the remainder of the school year."

I sat at my desk hoping Mr. Stanley would walk out the door and disappear forever. But that's not what happened. Instead, he smiled and said, "Hi, gang."

No one answered.

That's because he was supposed to say, "Good morning, class."

And we were supposed to answer, "Good morning, Mr. Stanley."

Ms Horton left the room. I could feel the air warming up. *O Canada* came ringing into the room. Everyone stood up to sing. Mr. Stanley sounded like a bullfrog. I started to giggle. I didn't mean to — it just happened. I looked around. The other kids were giggling too.

After *O Canada,* we sat down at our desks. Mr. Stanley passed around name tags. I wrote TARA MORGAN in tiny hearts with my neon pink marker. When I finished, my name tag looked awesome. I stuck it on my T-shirt.

Mr. Stanley was standing at the front of the room with a big smile on his face. "Before we begin," he said, "are there any questions?"

Jason Miles waved his hand in the air.

"Yes, Jason?" Mr. Stanley said.

"Have you ever counted all the freckles on your face?"

"No," Mr. Stanley said. "But thank you for noticing them. I'm quite proud of my freckles. I think they make a person's face look all dressed up."

Cory looked up and smiled. He had freckles all over his face too.

"Now, any more questions?" Mr. Stanley asked. No hands went up. "Okey-dokey," he said, "let's get straight to work."

Mr. Stanley got the morning completely mixed up. We were in the middle of sponge painting when Madame Gascon, the French teacher, knocked on the door.

"*Bonjour*," she said cheerfully. But her happy face disappeared when she noticed the paint smeared up our arms. It took us ten minutes to clean up. Then we had to rush through the French lesson.

After French, we were supposed to do math. But instead Mr. Stanley said, "Time for a Brain Drain!"

He divided the class into groups of three. He gave each group a pile of newspapers and a roll of masking tape.

"This is a contest!" he announced, rubbing his hands together. "Let's see which group can build the highest tower. You may use three things: newspaper, masking tape and your hands."

That's all he said! He didn't give us any instructions.

Jason and Cory were in my group. No matter how we taped the papers together, our tower kept flopping over.

"This is impossible!" I grumbled. "The only

thing these newspapers are good for is making paper airplanes."

I was busy making a supersonic missile when Jason poked me. "Look at Melissa's group," he said, his eyes widening.

I dropped my missile. Their tower was almost as high as the ceiling. They were rolling pieces of newspaper into tubes. Then they were sticking one end of each tube inside another and taping the joints. Melissa was holding the bottom of the tower with her hands.

"Hey, no fair!" I cried out, "Melissa's holding the tower up with her hands."

"You weren't listening," Mr. Stanley said. "I said, build a tower using newspaper, masking tape and your hands."

"Oh, yeah," I said, feeling my face turn red. "I forgot."

When each group had finished building a tower, Mr. Stanley looked pleased. He stood up and said, "Today you built a tower out of newspaper. Who knows? Maybe someday you'll build a bridge out of steel."

Chapter 2

Best Friends

At lunch I sat with Tam Ho. Tam sits next to me in class. She's my next door neighbour and my best friend. Even though Tam and I are best friends, we're very different. Tam's hair is black as midnight and straight as spaghetti. Mine is strawberry blond and curly all over, like a French poodle.

Of all the kids in grade three, including the boys, I'm the tallest. Tam's the shortest. My eyes are light blue. Hers are dark brown. And that's not all: we were even born in different parts of the world. I was born in Canada, and I still live in Canada. Tam was born in a country called Vietnam. When she was six years old, her family moved to Canada.

When I first met Tam, she spoke Vietnamese. Imagine, moving to Canada and not being able to speak English or French! The Ho family arrived in the summer. Right away they went to a special school to learn English. And I taught Tam the kind of things they don't teach you in school — like how to dress and talk cool.

My stomach growled. I opened my lunch box. The usual: a peanut butter sandwich, milk, an orange and a chocolate-chip granola bar.

I glanced over at Tam's lunch. Oh yuck. Her mom always packed sickening lunches. I watched as she was about to stick a pastry in her mouth. She took a bite. Yellow and green mush oozed out the sides of it.

"Eew," I said, pointing at the mush. "That's gross."

"No, it's not," she said. "It's delicious. Want to try?" She stuck it right under my nose.

"No way!" I said, pushing her hand away. "I don't eat anything green or yellow that's mushy."

"Oh, yeah? What about bananas? And what about green slushies? I thought they were your favourite."

Tam wasn't catching on too fast, so I pointed straight at her lunch and said, "I mean, I don't eat anything that looks like that!"

Tam put her hands on her hips. She narrowed her eyes and bunched up her lips. "You've never even tried it. You can't say you don't like it."

"Yes I can. It's yucky."

"No it's not. It's yummy."

"Yucky!"

"Yummy!"

"Yucky!"

"Yummy!"

"Okay, okay," I said. "Truce. You eat your lunch and I'll try not to look because if I do I'll throw up."

I stuffed my sandwich into my mouth. My tongue got completely stuck with peanut butter. I couldn't have talked even if I had wanted to. Next, I peeled the skin off my orange. When I heard Tam crunch on an apple, I knew it was safe. So I turned and said, "I miss Mrs. Jay already."

"Me too," she said.

"Can you believe the new teacher?" I said. "He's such a geek."

Tam put her apple down and frowned at me.

"What's wrong?" I said. "Why are you looking at me that way?"

"Mr. Stanley just dresses a little weird," Tam said. "And it's not easy being the new person at school. I should know. When I moved here, I thought I'd never fit in."

It was true. Tam had some strange ideas when she first moved to Canada.

"Remember when we were in grade one?" I said, laughing. "Right in the middle of Reading you stood up and began to scream that rice was falling from the sky."

"How was I supposed to know?" Tam said.

"I'd never seen snow in Vietnam. And Miss Santos didn't mind. She rushed me straight outside to feel the snow. It felt so soft and cold in my hands."

"But then you wouldn't come back to the class. You hid in the washroom for about an hour."

"That's because I felt so stupid. All the kids were laughing at me."

"Well!" I exclaimed, tossing my hands in the air. "What did you expect? You were running around screaming about rice falling from the sky."

"But I really believed it."

"Oh, yeah. Wasn't there some story about a dragon?"

"Not just any old dragon. When we lived in Vietnam, my father used to tell me a story about a greedy dragon. At night it would swoop down from the sky and eat all the rice from the paddies. He told me that one day its stomach would get so full it would burst open, and all the rice would rain down over the world."

"And you believed that?"

"When you're hungry you have to believe. Every day in Vietnam I watched for the falling rice. It never came. And then, that day in grade one . . ."

"Yeah," I said, "but back to Mr. Stanley. You see, it's different with him. Being a geek is not the same as coming from a different country. You acted dumb because you didn't know any better. Now you do."

I bit into my orange. It squirted me in the eye.

"Mr. Stanley has feelings too," Tam snapped.

Sometimes Tam gets touchy about things.

"Okay," I said, just to make her happy. "I'll give Mr. Stanley a chance."

Chapter 3

A Strange Afternoon

After lunch I put my Science notebook on top of my desk. Mrs. Jay had been teaching us about life at the seashore.

Mr. Stanley walked into the classroom. "Books away, please," he said. "Then line up at the door. Class will be held outside today. This is the perfect time of year to get in tune with the environment."

Cory rushed to stand first in line. Cory always

has to be first.

One by one we marched out of Riverside School. We crossed the street and walked four blocks to Riverview Park.

Riverview Park is beautiful. It has a huge grassy meadow with lots of picnic tables. There's a jungle gym with four slides, six swings, a tire that spins, monkey bars, a sandbox and a Tarzan rope. At the far end of the park is a pine forest. Deep in the forest is a shallow river that rushes over slippery rocks.

We walked into the forest and stopped by the banks of the river. Mr. Stanley told us to form a circle. He stood in the middle.

"Today we're going to make music in the woods," he said. That's all he said. Then he closed his eyes.

All at once, Laura Allen started waving her hands in the air. "Uh, uh, uh," she grunted.

Mr. Stanley didn't answer. He was facing the other way, and his eyes were still closed.

Finally, she yelled to get his attention. "Mr. Stanley!"

He turned and opened his eyes.

Laura stepped forward, tossing her golden ringlets in the air. "Mrs. Bell is the music teacher," she told him. "She comes on Tuesday and Thursday afternoons. We never have music on Mondays."

"Things are going to be a little different from now on," Mr. Stanley said.

Different! I didn't want things to be different. I wanted grade three to be normal again.

"Okey-dokey," Mr. Stanley said. "Now class, close your eyes." He began to croak a song. I pinched myself so I wouldn't laugh out loud. But nothing could stop me from laughing on the inside.

"Listen, listen, what do you hear?" Mr. Stanley stood like a statue with one ear stuck to the sky. Suddenly he pointed a finger at . . . absolutely nothing. "I hear a leaf drop over there."

Then he turned to Cory and sang, "Cory, Cory, what do you hear?"

"Nothing," Cory said.

"Listen again," Mr. Stanley said. "Try closing your eyes. It'll help you to concentrate."

"I don't hear anything," Cory insisted, digging the heels of his hightops into the ground.

I didn't hear anything either.

Poor Cory. Mr. Stanley wouldn't leave him alone. "Cory, Cory, what do you hear?"

Finally, Cory blurted out, "The wind, I guess."

"Good answer," Mr. Stanley said. "And what does the wind sound like?"

Cory's face was bright red. There were two deep grooves in the ground by his feet. "The wind sounds like the wind. That's all!"

"Can anyone help?" Mr. Stanley asked.

Tam stuck out her lips. "Whooo-ooo-ahooo."

Mr. Stanley clapped his hands. "Excellent. Tam sounds just like a soft breeze."

After that Mr. Stanley made us chirp like the birds in the forest. Then he made us bubble like the river flowing over rocks. Next he divided up the class. Some of us made wind sounds.

Some of us made river sounds. The rest of us made bird sounds. In the end, we put all the sounds together. Mr. Stanley called our sounds "nature's music." It was a very strange afternoon. But what else should I have expected from a very strange teacher?

After school, I walked home with Tam.

"Told you so," I said. "I gave Mr. Stanley a chance to prove that he's normal. Instead he proved that he's a major geek."

Tam folded her arms. "I had fun," she said.

There was no use talking to Tam about Mr. Stanley. She didn't understand.

* * *

By the time I arrived home from school it was four o'clock. My stomach was growling: "Feed me! Feed me! Feed me!"

Mom pulled in the driveway behind me, right on time. Her job at the bank ends at three-thirty every day, so we get home at the same time. I'm glad, since it's just Mom and me in our family.

I headed straight for the kitchen and gobbled up three oatmeal cookies. Then I poured myself a glass of cold milk. Yummy! My stomach gurgled: "Thank you! Thank you! Thank you!"

Mom asked me the same old after-school questions. "How was school, dear?"

"Fine."

"Anything new today?"

I almost said "Nope," because that's what I usually say. But suddenly I remembered I had a ton of new things to tell her.

First I told her about Mrs. Jay having the baby. She asked all sorts of questions, like "How much does the baby weigh?" and "When is he coming home from the hospital?"

I said, "How should I know?"

Next I told her about Mr. Stanley. "He's really weird. A geek."

Mom got this strange look on her face. "Why do you call him a geek?"

"Well, you see," I explained, "he's got frizzy yellow hair and yellow glasses to match. He wears weird clothes, and he does weird stuff. You know, geeky stuff."

Mom shook her head. "I don't approve of such language. It can be very hurtful to others."

"But Mom, everyone uses the word geek. It's even in the dictionary."

"That doesn't mean I have to like it," she said sternly. "At the very least, you should give Mr. Stanley a chance. Get to know him before you decide he's a geek."

Mom was sounding a lot like Tam. That bugged me.

It wasn't my fault that Mr. Stanley was a geek.

Chapter 4

Monster Bug

The next morning our class visited the school library. Mr. Stanley had a long list of books for us to find: spider books, wildflower books, insect books, weed books, rodent books, bird books, tree books.

I cornered Mr. Stanley by the encyclopedias. "Why do we need so many books?" I asked.

"We're going to do something a little different today," he told me.

Uh oh. There was that word "different" again.

In the afternoon, Mr. Stanley told the class to line up at the door. Cory rushed to be first in line, but Laura beat him. So he tried to push her out of his spot.

"Hey, watch it," she snapped. "I don't want your cooties all over my taffeta dress. It cost a lot of money, you know."

"Who cares about your Daffy Duck dress?" he sneered.

"It's taffeta! And keep your hands off it."

Just then Mr. Stanley joined the line. He was carrying a small suitcase. "Follow me," he said.

One by one we marched out of Riverside school. We crossed the street and walked four blocks to Riverview Park. We walked past the meadow, past the picnic tables, past the jungle gym, and we didn't stop until we had reached the river.

Everyone, except for Laura, sat cross-legged in a circle on the ground. Laura stood the whole time so she wouldn't get dirt on her taffeta dress.

Mr. Stanley opened the suitcase. Inside were all the library books. "Okey-dokey," he said, "today we're going to play I Spy."

I leaned over to Tam and whispered, "A baby game!"

Mr. Stanley looked straight at me. "Tara, you may start the game."

All the others had to close their eyes. Then Mr. Stanley said, "Tara, look all around. You have three minutes to discover something that you've never seen before."

I looked up to the sky. I looked down to the ground. I looked across the river. And in the trees. Then I saw it, right in front of me. A monster bug. It was longer than my longest finger. It had a dragon's head and eyes that bulged out like ping-pong balls. No wonder I hadn't noticed it before. It was exactly the same shade of green as the leaf it was sitting on. And its wings looked like little leaves.

Mr. Stanley handed me the insect book. "Now, Tara, name that thing."

The rest of the kids were getting bored. So I

turned the pages quickly. There it was! On page thirty-two. I got so excited, I could hardly wait to finish the game. I turned to the class and said, "I spy with my little eye, a praying mantis."

They all opened their eyes. Laura pointed to a purple wildflower. "Is that a praying mantis?"

"Nope," I said.

Jason pointed to a minnow in the river. "Is that a praying mantis?"

"No again," I said.

Everyone had a turn. And everyone guessed wrong. Even Melissa. And Melissa hardly ever guesses wrong.

At last I pointed to the leaf. All at once, everyone saw the bug. There were lots of "oohs" and "aahs" and "wows."

We played I Spy for the whole afternoon. I learned about water striders, trilliums, indigo buntings and fairy-steps.There were so many things in the forest I had never noticed before. I guess I had never really looked.

After school Mom asked, "How was school, dear?"

"Fine."

"Anything new today?"

"Yup. We played I Spy in the park."

Mom raised her eyebrows. "Aren't you a bit old for I Spy?"

"It wasn't the baby kind of I Spy," I said. "It was so cool." I explained the game to Mom while I spread crunchy peanut butter on crackers.

The doorbell rang. It was Tam. I stuffed the crackers into my mouth, and we went to play at her house.

The outside of Tam's house looks just like mine: a white bungalow with green shutters and a green front door. But inside, our houses are very different. Tam and her six-year-old sister Loan share one bedroom. Her grandfather sleeps in the other bedroom. Her mother and father sleep in a bedroom in the basement.

One time I asked Tam, "Doesn't it drive you crazy — so many people living inside one tiny house?"

She laughed. Then she told me about her

home in Vietnam. Her whole family had lived in one little room. They had to eat, sleep and play in the same room. I made up my mind right then and there to quit complaining to Mom that our house was too small.

We played with Tam's giant-sized ball. I had so much fun, until Tam asked me to stay for dinner. Again! I was getting sick of making excuses.

"Uh . . . I can't," I told her. "I have to go home and feed my goldfish."

It wasn't really a lie. I did have to feed my goldfish. But the truth is I would throw up if I had to eat sheep's eyeballs and chocolate-covered ants for dinner.

How did I know that's what Mrs. Ho would serve? I didn't. But I was very suspicious. Melissa (who knows just about everything) told the class that people in some faraway country eat sheep's eyeballs for dinner and chocolate-covered ants for dessert. What if that country was Vietnam? I couldn't take the chance.

Chapter 5

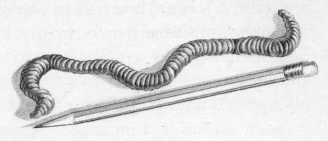

The Big Fight

The week that followed was full of new and exciting activities. I never knew what to expect at school. That was part of the fun. I guess you could say I had finally gotten used to Mr. Stanley. Anyway, my life was going great — but then something happened that messed it all up.

One night, thunder crashed through the city. Hail the size of jawbreakers knocked on my windowpane. Bright orange and yellow streaks lit up the sky. What an excellent storm!

By morning the rain had changed to drizzle. Tam and I walked to school in our raincoats and rubber boots. We splashed through every puddle. It's a good thing I was watching the ground, or else I might have squashed the worm that was stretched across the sidewalk. This wasn't just any old worm: it was the longest, juiciest worm I had ever seen. It was as long as a brand-new pencil.

When Tam saw the worm, she jumped back. "Eew, disgusting!" she cried.

The worm wasn't disgusting. It was amazing. I bent down for a closer look. It wasn't moving.

"Maybe it's sick," I told Tam. "The rain probably filled its burrow. And the poor thing doesn't know how to swim. It's probably half-drowned."

Tam's face puckered up like she had just swallowed a whole box of Super Sour candies. "Forget about the stupid worm. You're making us late for school."

I was about to say goodbye to the worm. But then I saw a robin circling overhead. It was hungry for worm stew.

"Move along," I told the worm. "Hurry back to your burrow. A fat robin wants to eat you for breakfast."

The worm didn't move. I tried to push it. But it wouldn't budge.

Well, I couldn't just leave a helpless worm alone on the sidewalk with a robin nearby, so I picked it up.

"Isn't it cute?" I said, giving Tam a closer look.

"Don't come near me," she warned, stepping back. "I hate worms."

"Worms are nice," I told her. "They can't hurt you."

Tam kept backing up. "Didn't you hear me? I HATE WORMS!"

I wanted Tam to see how beautiful the worm was, so I dangled it right in front of her eyes.

"Get that creepy-crawler away from me," she ordered in a super sour voice.

"It's not a creepy-crawler," I said. "It's a cute

squirmy-wormy."

"You're gross to pick up a worm."

"Don't call me gross!"

"Gross! Gross! Gross!"

"I AM NOT GROSS!" Suddenly something inside me exploded, and I threw the worm at Tam. "Catch!" I cried.

The worm hit her raincoat, stuck for a second, then slid to the ground.

The next thing I knew she was screaming and bawling at the same time. But I could still make out her words: "I hate you, Tara!"

Then, all of a sudden, she turned and ran to school. Without me.

Chapter 6

This Worm Is Sick

I crawled through the grass and found the worm. "Are you okay?" I said, checking to make sure it was still in one piece.

"Sorry I threw you at Tam. I didn't mean to . . . but she made me so angry. Just because I happen to like worms, she called me gross. And she called you a creepy-crawler. How dare she! To me, you look like the king of the worms."

I stroked the worm gently with one finger. "I think I'll call you Wallace. Wallace is a name fit for a king."

Cupping Wallace safely in my hands, I headed for school. When I reached the schoolyard, Cory ran up to me. "What's that in your hands?" he asked.

I showed him the worm.

His eyes popped out. "Awesome!" He reached deep into his jeans pocket and brought out a piece of red licorice. It was covered with blue lint.

"Trade you," he said.

"No way," I answered.

He reached into his pocket again. "How about two pieces?"

"I don't want to trade," I insisted. "This worm is sick. I'm taking him to Mr. Stanley."

Cory eyed Wallace closely. "That worm doesn't look sick. It looks dead!"

"He's NOT dead! I told you, he's just sick."

The bell rang. Everywhere, kids were running to their classrooms. I walked slowly so Wallace wouldn't get hurt again.

By the time I reached the classroom, most of the kids were sitting at their desks. I kicked off my boots. But I got stuck in my raincoat. Hmm . . . how could I hold onto Wallace and get out of my raincoat at the same time? I called Laura to help me. She looked the other way. So I called Melissa. She looked the other way too. Why were they acting so strange?

I couldn't just stand in front of my locker all day. So I bunched Wallace in one hand. Then I twisted and bounced until my raincoat dropped to the floor.

When I sat down at my desk, I looked over at Tam. She scowled back at me. Her eyes were red and puffy.

Mr. Stanley walked into the room. He was wearing a purple polka-dot shirt and green pants. He smiled at the class and said, "Hi, gang."

And we answered, "Hi, Mr. Stanley."

I rushed up to Mr. Stanley and opened my hands. He stared down at Wallace. "That's a fine-looking earthworm," he said. "But it doesn't belong at school. Take it outside, please."

"But he's sick," I said. "Could you help him? Pretty please, with chocolate sprinkles on top?" Normally I don't like to beg, but this was important.

Mr. Stanley must like chocolate sprinkles because he smiled and said, "May I hold him?"

"Sure," I said, dropping it into his hands. "His name is Wallace."

Behind his yellow lenses Mr. Stanley's eyes were buzzing around, studying the worm. I held my breath. Finally he looked up. "Wallace is pretty special, eh?"

"Very special," I said.

"Well, Tara, I can't promise to make him better, but I'll try."

I almost jumped up and hugged him. Then I remembered I was at school.

Mr. Stanley grabbed a large pickle jar from the classroom closet and rushed out the door.

Before we had finished singing *O Canada*, he was back. The pickle jar was filled with dirt, pebbles, grass, leaves and Wallace. With a screwdriver, Mr. Stanley poked holes in the lid.

"Earthworms like the dark," he told the class. "This guy will be happy in the closet for now. After lunch, we'll have a closer peek."

I heard Tam whisper the word "gross" to Laura. I wished that I had never taught her that word.

Our class was very busy that morning. We did two pages of fractions. We wrote in our journals. (I wrote about finding Wallace and Tam being mad at me.) Laura read out loud in reading circle. We had French with Madame Gascon.

By recess the sun was shining outside. But it was still cloudy and drizzly inside me. Tam was playing with Laura and Melissa. All around me, kids were running and kicking balls and playing hopscotch. I was standing all alone.

Suddenly I felt a tap on my shoulder. I turned around. It was Laura. She was pointing her pink polished fingernail at me. Melissa and Tam were standing beside her.

"That was a rotten thing you did to Tam," she said, jabbing her fingernail at my nose.

"Worm lover," Melissa sneered.

Tam didn't say anything. She shot me a dirty look instead. Then they skipped off, chanting:

Tara, Tara, you're so gross,
We don't want to get too close!
Kissing, kissing all the worms,
Now you've got their dirty germs!

Recess is only fifteen minutes long. But when you're alone and your friends have turned against you, recess lasts forever. I leaned against the school wall. This is how it felt to be the most unpopular kid in Riverside School. Worse than infected chicken pox. Worse than being grounded for a month. Worse than Christmas without presents. I wished I had never found the worm in the first place.

After lunch Mr. Stanley got the pickle jar from the closet. Wallace was limp. He hadn't moved one centimetre. I could tell Mr. Stanley was worried by the way he was tapping his toe on the floor. "If the worm hasn't moved by tomorrow," he said, "I'm not sure he's going to live."

I had already lost my best friend. Now Wallace might die. Ouch! A double whammy.

Chapter 7

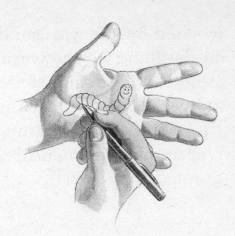

Me and Mr. Stanley

How could I concentrate on school work? All I could think about was Tam and Wallace — and how I'd wrecked everything. My pen started to doodle a picture of Wallace on my hand.

"Tara," Mr. Stanley said, "Please pay attention."

I dropped the pen and looked up to see the pickle jar being passed from desk to desk.

Wallace was being called things like awesome, disgusting, gross, radical and slime ball. When the jar reached Tam's desk, she refused to look at Wallace. She plugged her nose and passed the jar to the next desk.

Jason shot his arm in the air. "Uh, uh, uh," he grunted.

Finally he got Mr. Stanley's attention. "There's this friend of mine who eats bugs," Jason said. "Fried crickets are his favourite. He says they taste like peanuts."

Mr. Stanley didn't look surprised at all. "Insects can be quite nutritious. Every bit as good for you as chicken or fish."

Yuck, first sheep's eyeballs and chocolate-covered ants. Now, fried crickets. Why can't people just stick with cheese pizza?

Mr. Stanley put Wallace back in the closet. "Tomorrow, we'll have a special science lesson starring the earthworm," he said. "That is, if it's still alive."

After school I walked home alone. I missed Tam so much. She had never been mad at me for a whole day before. This had been the worst day of my life!

When I got home, I wasn't hungry. I watched TV until Mom called me for dinner. After dinner I went straight to my room and stared at my goldfish for the rest of the night.

The next morning I walked to school alone. I didn't sing *O Canada*. Mr. Stanley frowned at me. I didn't read out loud in reading circle. Mr. Stanley frowned at me again. I left the page blank in my journal. Mr. Stanley frowned at me again. I didn't care.

The recess bell rang. Tam, Laura and Melissa were making recess plans as they dashed out the door. Mr. Stanley made me stay inside. When we were alone, he called me to his desk. He was tapping his foot on the floor. *Tap, tap, tap.*

"What's wrong, Tara?"

"Nothing."

"The Tara I know sings *O Canada* with gusto."

I wasn't sure what gusto meant. But I didn't feel like asking.

"The Tara I know loves to read out loud in reading circle."

Tap, tap, tap went his foot.

"The Tara I know writes wonderful stories in her journal."

Tap, tap, tap.

I couldn't speak. My chin was quivering. I figured if I opened my mouth I'd start bawling.

Chapter 8

The Amazing Earthworm

Mr. Stanley stared right through me, as though he was trying to suck the answer out of my brain. Finally, he said, "Are you an alien invader? Have you possessed Tara's body?"

I couldn't believe my ears. What was he talking about?

"Alien, what have you done with Tara? She's one of my best students. I want her back."

Mr. Stanley was acting so silly. I couldn't help

myself — I started to laugh. "It's me, Tara Morgan!"

Mr. Stanley wiped his brow. "Whew, is it really you?"

"You knew it was me all along," I said.

"Just checking," he said, winking. "You can't be too sure these days. There's no room in my class for aliens. I'm only trained to teach earthlings."

Suddenly his face turned serious. "So tell me. What's wrong?"

"I think I killed the worm."

"Come with me," he said. I followed him to the closet. He brought out the pickle jar and held it in front of my eyes. "See for yourself."

I looked in the jar. Wallace was gone. My legs turned to marshmallow. I swallowed hard, then sputtered, "Did you bury Wallace?"

"Wallace buried himself," Mr. Stanley said. "Look again." He pointed to the side of the jar. Wallace was busy making a tunnel in the dirt.

"Neato!" I exclaimed, trying to sound excited. But I still could not make myself smile.

"Uh oh, something's still bothering you."

"You can't help me with my other problem."

"Is it Tam?"

"Yeah. She hates me. How did you know?"

"I read your journal yesterday."

"Oh, yeah. You know the whole story. Hitting her with a worm was such a dumb thing to do."

"Have you apologized?"

"I can't. Tam won't speak to me. She won't even look at me."

"That's too bad," Mr. Stanley said. "Hang in there. Good friends usually find a way of working things out."

Talking to Mr. Stanley made me feel a lot better. Best of all, he let me stay inside for the whole recess. I could not have faced my ex-friends singing "Tara, Tara, you're so gross" again.

After recess Mr. Stanley began the science lesson. He took Wallace out of the pickle jar and placed him on the table. Then he handed Jason a magnifying glass. "Look closely at the earthworm," he said. "I want you to find its eyes."

Jason looked at one end of Wallace. He looked at the other end. Then, with a dirty finger, he rolled Wallace over. Poor Wallace.

After Jason had flipped Wallace every which way, he put down the magnifying glass and looked up, puzzled. "This worm doesn't have any eyes. It doesn't have ears or a nose either. But I did find a tiny mouth."

"Well done," Mr. Stanley said, "You may return to your desk."

Mr. Stanley looked around the class. "Who can tell me how the earthworm moves?"

"Muscles," Melissa answered.

"Correct," Mr. Stanley said. "An earthworm has rings of muscle around its body. These muscles push and pull to move it through the dirt. Since the worm has no bones, it can bend into any shape — even tie itself into a knot."

"Cool," said Jason, wiping his chin with his shirtsleeve.

Mr. Stanley held Wallace up in the air. "This animal has no eyes, no nose, no ears, no arms, no legs and no bones. What is it good for?"

Cory raised his hand. "Bait! I'm in the business. I catch them and sell them. A loonie a dozen. Best price in town. And guaranteed to catch a fish."

Yikes! All of a sudden, I knew why Cory wanted to trade his linty licorice for Wallace. He wanted to sell my worm for bait.

"Anyone else know what earthworms are good for?" Mr. Stanley asked.

No hands went up. Mr. Stanley explained that worms are like tiny plows that break up the dirt to let air and water reach the plants' roots. They eat leaves and grass and turn them into rich garden soil.

Mr. Stanley put Wallace back in the jar. He called Tam and me to the front of the room. "I want you girls to watch the worm closely," he said. "Tell me when it starts to burrow. The rest of you, read quietly at your desks for now."

Mr. Stanley winked at me. I got the message. This was my chance to apologize to Tam.

Chapter 9

A Second Chance

Tam refused to budge from her desk. "I can't!" she whimpered. "I'm allergic to worms."

What a dumb excuse!

Mr. Stanley didn't believe her either. "You don't have to touch the worm," he told her. "Just look at it."

"Do I have to?"

"Yes," Mr. Stanley said firmly.

Tam dragged herself to the front of the room.

She stood next to me, but she didn't look at me and she didn't look at Wallace. She stared down at her shoes.

It's now or never, I told myself. Tam has to listen. Mr. Stanley won't let her walk away.

"I'm sorry I threw the worm at you," I said. "It was a stupid thing to do."

"You should be sorry," Tam said, still staring at her shoes.

"I'll never, ever do it again," I said. "Promise, cross my eyes and hope to eat snake liver. Can we be friends again?"

"Maybe," she said. At least she didn't say no.

A few minutes later Wallace started to burrow. The class gathered around to watch. Wallace pushed tiny pebbles and dirt out of his way until he had disappeared deep into the jar. Then Mr. Stanley put the jar back in the closet.

After school I walked home alone. It looked like Tam's "maybe" had really meant "no."

Somehow Mom guessed that I was miserable. Maybe it was because I couldn't stop crying.

She sat beside me on the couch. Between sobs, I told her about finding Wallace and about having the biggest fight of my life with Tam.

"I'm sure you've done your best to make up with Tam," Mom said. "And I'm sure Tam will forgive you sooner or later."

I wished I could be so sure.

That night Mom cooked one of my favourite dinners: tacos with no onions in the hamburger. For dessert she brought a chocolate cake out of the freezer.

All night Mom was extra nice. She tried to made me smile by telling goofy riddles like:

Knock, knock.

Who's there?

Boo.

Boo who?

Don't cry, Tara. Things will get better soon.

They didn't. The weekend was BORING! Saturday morning I helped Mom clean the house. Then we walked to the mall to buy a new shower curtain. Like I said, boring. Mom bought me a new jigsaw puzzle. I chose a five-hundred-piece puzzle with super small pieces. I figured it would take forever to put it together. Perfect. I had forever.

All Sunday afternoon I worked on the puzzle. It was a picture of a bunch of kids riding on a Ferris wheel. They were screaming and laughing, having a wonderful time. Every puzzle piece was different. Yet each was a perfect fit. I was creating a world of happy faces. If only it was that easy to fit into the real world.

Later, Mom asked me to go strawberry picking. I was glad. I couldn't stand looking at all those happy faces any more. We drove a long way down a dirt road, then turned at a sign that read: U-Pick Strawberries. We filled two baskets. That night we made a batch of strawberry jam together.

I was dreading Monday morning — the beginning of the last week of school. I thought about staying home sick all week. But then I'd never get a chance to fix things up with my friends. And over the long summer they'd probably forget that Tara Morgan ever existed.

So there I was, back at school on Monday morning. Tam, Melissa and Laura ignored me all day. On Tuesday they ignored me again. By Wednesday I was sort of getting used to being ignored. At least they had stopped chanting that awful rhyme.

Thursday morning, I was getting dressed for school when the doorbell rang.

Yippee! I thought. Tam's forgiven me.

I raced down the hall and threw open the door. Rats! It was Mrs. Cooper from down the street. Her car wouldn't start, and she needed Mom to give her a lift to work.

"Come in," I said. "Mom will be ready in a minute." I tried hard to smile at Mrs. Cooper as I closed the door.

"Wait," a voice called. I opened the door. Mrs. Ho was running up the walk. Tam was right behind her.

My heart started pounding. I was afraid Mrs. Ho was going to yell at me. But she didn't. She smiled sweetly and invited me to dinner.

Uh oh! Big trouble! If I said no, I'd blow my

chance of being friends with Tam again. If I said yes, eew! — sheep's eyeballs and chocolate-covered ants!

"Sure, sounds great," I lied, swallowing back the lump in my throat. Then I got a brilliant idea. "I'll bring a special dessert," I told Mrs. Ho. "To make up for what I did."

"That's not necessary," she said.

"Please," I begged. And I kept on begging until she said yes. At least now I could cross chocolate-covered ants off the menu.

Tam walked to school with me. She didn't say much. I couldn't think of much to say either. But I was glad she was there.

At school I sang *O Canada* with gusto. Mr. Stanley smiled at me. During reading circle I read out loud. Mr. Stanley smiled at me again. In my journal I wrote about getting my best friend back. Best of all, at recess, Tam, Melissa, Laura and I played soccer together, and no one called me "worm lover."

After school, Mom drove me to the grocery store to buy the ingredients for the special dessert.

It was four o'clock already, and I was supposed to be at Tam's house by six. I ran up and down the aisles, grabbing this, grabbing that, waiting in a long line-up, paying the man, rushing home, mixing this, mixing that, pouring this, pouring that . . . whoops! cleaning up this . . . whoops! cleaning up that, whipping it together, adding sprinkles. . . . Presto! Blammo! A masterpiece!

Even Mom was impressed. "I bet Tam's family has never eaten anything quite like this," she said.

"It's going to be a big surprise," I told her.

Carefully, I placed the dessert inside a plastic container. But before I closed the lid, I tossed six juicy worms on top.

A wicked laugh arose in my throat. Perfect, I told myself.

Chapter 10

Vietnamese Dinner

Mrs. Ho greeted me at the front door. She was wearing a Vietnamese outfit called an *ao dai*. It's a long silky shirt over pants. Her long black hair was pulled back into a tight bun. She looked beautiful.

"Hi, Mrs. Ho," I said, handing her the dessert. "This has to go into the freezer right away."

She smiled at me. "What have you made?"

"It's a surprise for Tam," I said, grinning.

"Promise you won't tell?"

Mrs. Ho's eyes lit up. "Tam loves surprises. Your secret is safe with me."

I leaned over and whispered in her ear. "Worm Pie."

Mrs. Ho's mouth fell open. I could see all the way to the back of her throat. "Tara, you know how Tam feels about worms," she said. "Friendship is special. Tam may not forgive you a second time."

"Tam's my best friend," I said. "I wouldn't dare mess things up again."

Just then Tam came running around the corner. "Hi, I was in the living room playing cards with my grandfather. Come on, I'll deal you in."

"Cards will have to wait," Mrs. Ho said. "Dinner's ready."

Tam helped her grandfather to the table. He was very old and very short and super skinny and completely bald.

Mrs. Ho called Tam to the kitchen. The grandfather and I were left alone in the dining room. I couldn't think of anything to say. And he couldn't speak English very well. So we smiled a lot at each other. Did I ever feel strange! I wanted to be back home with Mom, eating tacos and laughing at her silly riddles.

After a few minutes had passed, Mr. Ho walked into the dining room carrying a soup tureen. Tam, Loan and Mrs. Ho followed. Then everyone sat down.

Mr. Ho served the soup. He placed a full bowl right in front of me. Oh, no! My worst nightmare was coming true. Chunks were floating in the soup! I hate chunks! They taste so . . . so . . . chunky.

First I stabbed around with my fork to make sure nothing was alive. Then I dipped my spoon into the warm broth. It tasted sweet and sour at the same time.

"Do you like the *canh chua*?" Mr. Ho asked.

"It's yummy," I lied.

I scooped up a chunk of soggy tomato and shoved it in my mouth. All of a sudden, I started to gag. Before anyone could notice, I took a big drink of water and washed the tomato down. Next I spooned up something white. Maybe it was fish. Or maybe it was something else! When the chunk hit my mouth, I started to gag again. I took another big drink of water and washed it all down.

"Excuse me," I said, "could I please have another glass of water? I'm very thirsty. In fact, I'll probably need a pitcher."

The whole family stared at me as though my hair had turned green. So I explained.

"Mom likes me to drink eight glasses of water a day . . . because . . . my body is mostly made out of water. I'll shrivel up like a prune if I don't drink lots and lots of water."

Mrs. Ho nodded politely. She filled a large pitcher of water and placed it smack in front of me. Now I had the courage to eat the yellow blob that was floating in the soup. I sucked it back. It was pineapple. Yes! I love pineapple! I fished out all the pineapple pieces and gobbled them right down.

When I had finished the soup, I let out a big sigh. I hadn't found one eyeball in the whole bowl.

Chapter 11

A Special Dessert

A lake was swishing around inside me. "May I be excused to go to the washroom?" I asked softly.

"Of course," Mrs. Ho said.

When I left the room, the family started talking in Vietnamese. I couldn't understand one word they were saying. But there were lots of giggles. I figured they were laughing at me. I didn't blame them. No one drinks that much water!

By the time I returned from the washroom, the soup dishes had been cleared. On the table was a large bowl of rice, a vegetable platter and a tray of meat.

Mr. Ho pointed to the meat. "This is *cha lua*. A special treat in Vietnam."

"What is *cha lua*?" I asked suspiciously.

"Pork with spices," he said.

That Melissa! I'd never listen to her again. I had been worried about sheep's eyeballs and chocolate-covered ants for no reason at all.

The Ho family ate their meal with chopsticks. Out of the corner of my eye, I watched Tam. She was an expert with the wooden sticks. She made it look so easy. The chopsticks looked like crab pincers snapping up the rice.

I grabbed a pair of chopsticks in one hand and tried to copy her. After poking around in my rice, I finally grabbed one measly grain. When I raised the chopsticks to my mouth, the grain fell back to my plate. Tam pointed to the knife and fork by my plate.

"Good idea," I said.

After the main course was finished, Mrs. Ho brought the dessert to the table. She looked very worried. "Are you sure about this?" she whispered to me.

"Yes," I said, "it will be lots of fun."

She placed the dessert in front of me. Then I stood up and said, "I'm really glad that Tam and I are best friends again. But there's still one problem: she doesn't like worms. Well, I'm going to change that tonight."

I grinned wickedly at Tam. She shot me the evil eye. The room was silent.

I uncovered the dessert and placed it right under her nose. "Ta dah! Worm pie!"

Tam screamed. "Ugh, worms! Crawling all over the pie! How could you!"

"Serves you right!" I said.

We stared straight into each other's eyes. Then we both cracked up laughing. Soon the whole family joined in.

"You're right," Tam said, "I do like worms — gummy worms."

"You had me very worried," said Mrs. Ho.

"Sorry," I told her. "I wanted to explain, but Tam walked into the room."

Mr. Ho was gazing down at the pie. "Interesting," he said. What's in it?"

"Lots of goodies," I said. "Chocolate cookies, whipped cream and chocolate pudding."

He looked like he was going to be sick.

"Don't worry," I said, "that's not real dirt on the top. And you can eat the worms — they're candy."

As it turned out, Mr. and Mrs. Ho were too full for dessert. And the grandfather couldn't have dessert. His stomach was too weak. But the rest of us loved the worm pie.

At eight o'clock Mom came to get me. Since the next day was the last day of school, she rushed me straight home.

"Wrap up Mr. Stanley's present," she said. "And don't dilly-dally. It's almost your bedtime."

I wrapped two jars of strawberry jam in pretty pink tissue paper and stuck a purple bow on top. Then I made Mr. Stanley a card.

Mr. Stanley, you are so cool.
Thanks for teaching me at school.
(If Wallace could speak he would thank you
too.)
From your student,
Tara Morgan.

That night I lay awake for a long, long time. There was so much to think about. There was always a party on the last day of school. Then it was summer vacation — yippee! — playing all day, staying up late and no school. I slept about two minutes the whole night.

Chapter 12

Surprise!

The next morning, Tam was at my door extra early. We ran all the way to school so we wouldn't miss any part of the last day.

When we arrived at the schoolyard, Jason was trying to play kissing tag. He was chasing the grade-three girls and knocking some of them down.

"Let's go tell the principal," I said to Tam. She nodded, and we marched to Ms Horton's office.

Six kids had already been sent to the principal's office that morning. They were all lined up on the bench outside.

We'd only been there a minute when Madame Gagnon arrived with Jason. She marched him straight to the front of the line. "I guess that takes care of that," Tam said.

I could see Ms Horton through the window in her office door. She was rubbing her forehead and looking sad. Suddenly I felt sorry for her. She sure had a lot of problems to fix. I reached into my backpack and ripped open Mr. Stanley's present. I took one of the jars of jam, stuck the purple bow on top of it . . . and left it by Ms Horton's door.

Just then the bell rang. Tam and I ran to class.

The best part about the last day of school was . . . everything! There was no work, just lots of games and lots of goodies to eat.

All morning long, Mr. Stanley kept hinting about a special surprise planned for the afternoon. Everyone tried to guess at what it could be.

Jason guessed, "A clown that does face-painting."

Melissa guessed, "Chocolate cake and ice cream."

Tam guessed, "A movie and popcorn."

I guessed, "A magic show."

We all guessed wrong. So it was a big surprise when Mrs. Jay walked through the door carrying baby Joel.

"Good afternoon, class," she said.

"Good afternoon, Mrs. Jay," we answered — just like old times.

It was great to see Mrs. Jay again. She still had that same sunny smile. But I felt kind of bad. Mrs. Jay had been my teacher for almost the whole year, and I didn't have a present for her.

When Joel fell asleep, Mrs. Jay visited us all at our desks. When she reached my desk, I handed her the other jar of jam.

"How nice," she said. "Strawberry's my favourite. How did you know?"

I shrugged. "A good guess."

Talking to Mrs. Jay made me feel good all

over. But soon Joel was awake and crying. A stinky odor filled the room. Pyew! All the kids were groaning and plugging their noses. Mrs. Jay said goodbye and rushed Joel out the door.

At the end of the day, Mr. Stanley brought Wallace out of the closet. I had been having so much fun, I had forgotten about the worm. Oops! What if he had been stuck at school for the whole summer?

"The earthworm is strong and healthy now," Mr. Stanley said. "It's time to set him free."

He handed me the pickle jar. "When you get home, let Wallace loose in your garden. That way you'll know that he's happy and helping your garden at the same time."

I didn't feel very happy about letting Wallace go. After all, I had saved him. And he would look awesome on my bedroom dresser. But deep down, I knew that Mr. Stanley was right. Wallace belonged in the ground with the rest of the worms. Who knows? Maybe he had a family waiting for him.

Before the bell rang, I gave Mr. Stanley his

card. "This is for you. I wanted to bring you a present, but — "

Before I could finish, Mr. Stanley started to read the poem out loud. When he stopped, his face turned red. I thought that only happened to kids.

"This card is very special. No one's ever called me cool before. Thanks, Tara."

Then the bell rang.

Yahoo! I picked up Wallace and grabbed Tam's hand, and we ran out the door. This was going to be the best summer ever.

Tara's Worm Pie Recipe

1	package instant chocolate pudding
250 mL	whipped topping
1	prepared chocolate pie shell
250 mL	chocolate cookie crumbs
6	gummy worms

1. Prepare the chocolate pudding according to the instructions on the box.
2. Fold the whipped topping into the pudding and mix them together until the filling is smooth.
3. Pour the filling into the pie shell and spread it evenly with a spatula.
4. Sprinkle the top of the pie with chocolate cookie crumbs. (This is the dirt.)
5. Top the whole thing off with gummy worms.

Chill the pie in the freezer until it's firm enough to slice. Serves 6.

Beverly Scudamore

A fan of the outdoors, Beverly Scudamore especially loves water sports like sailing, canoeing and swimming. When the water freezes, she loves to skate and cross-country ski. She has also always loved taking care of animals — even worms.

Beverly and her family live in Bright's Grove, Ontario. This is her first book.